SCAREDY Cat

For my dad who sparked my love of books and
for Pip — of course! HG
To Apple, Hari, and Bee. AT

First published in the UK in 2018.
This edition published in 2019
by New Frontier Publishing Europe Ltd
Uncommon, 126 New King's Road
Fulham, London SW6 4LZ
www.newfrontierpublishing.co.uk

ISBN: 978-1-912858-00-2

A CIP catalogue record for this book is available from
the British Library.

Printed in China
10 9 8 7 6 5 4 3 2

SCAREDY Cat

Heather Gallagher · Anil Tortop

NEW FRONTIER PUBLISHING

Have you seen my Scaredy Cat?
He's afraid of this and afraid of that!

Afraid of bees and ...

towering trees and ...

Granny's super-duper sneeze.

ACHOO!

Have you seen my Scaredy Cat?
He's afraid of this and afraid of that!

walking toys and ...

calling, sprawling, brawling boys.

costumed kids, striking poses.

Have you seen my Scaredy Cat?
He's afraid of this and afraid of that!

Afraid of muck and ...

chomping, chewing garbage trucks.

Have you seen my Scaredy Cat?
He's afraid of this and afraid of that!

leaping, creeping, crawling crooks.

But don't you worry, Scaredy Cat,
because I'm ...

BRAVE like this and BRAVE like that!

I'll chase those hooks and
stack those books and ...

Scaredy Cat, oh Scaredy Cat,

You're no simple, hissing moggie ...

You're my crazy, kissing doggie!
I love you, Scaredy Cat!